# Maddie Saves The Day

Jaclyn and Heidi Weist

Jaclyn
Weist

# Maddie Saves The Day

Jaclyn and Heidi Weist

Dragons & Fairy Tales Press

For Heidi ~ My real-life Maddie.
Never stop dreaming.
Never stop believing.
Never stop dancing.

# Chapter One

Maddie stared up at the clouds, trying to find the best shape in the sky. William had already found a rubber duck and a pirate ship, and she couldn't let him win.

"Come on, I'm bored." William stood and brushed the leaves off his shorts. "Let's go play with our swords."

"Not until I find a good cloud shape— oh look! Muffins is back!" Maddie hopped up and ran to the unicorn that used to be her pet until he decided to stay in the fairy world.

William made a face and stomped toward the fence. "I'm going to Michael's house."

Maddie hugged Muffins tightly. "He's just sad that I have another friend to play with. I missed you, Muffins. Why are you here?"

Muffins whinnied and nodded his head. Sparks of light showered down from his horn. Maddie jumped back. That had never happened before.

A small man dressed all in green appeared next to Muffins, nearly falling over. "Ah, Maddie. It is you."

"Eoin?" Maddie hadn't seen a leprechaun since her sister Megan's wedding.

"Aye. And I'm here to ask your help. Do you still have your wand from Jared?"

Maddie nodded. "It's in my room. Why do you need it?"

Eoin burst into tears. "All of the animals are trapped."

Maddie gasped. "Trapped? Who trapped them?"

"A dark fairy. She doesn't like animals, so she captured them all. Can you help me save them?" Eoin took off his hat, showing his messy hair underneath.

Maddie stared up at the house. Her mom was busy, and Megan was gone. It was the perfect time to go save the day.

"I'll get my wand and then meet you out here." Maddie started to run but stopped. "How are we going to get there?"

Eoin patted Muffins' back. "Muffins will take us."

# Chapter Two

Maddie stared at Eoin. "But Muffins is too small to take us."

"That's what we need your wand for. You can make him bigger."

"Oh!" Maddie ran into her house and found a small bag to put her clothes and shoes and favorite doll inside. She couldn't leave Mrs. Fluffykins at home. Maddie's wand went into the special belt that Jared had made for her.

Mommy wasn't in the kitchen when Maddie got downstairs, so she grabbed some snacks and then ran back outside where Eoin and Muffins stood.

"I'm ready." Maddie held out her wand and waved it in the air with her eyes closed.

"Hey, Maddie don't you think—" Eoin's voice was drowned out by the loud whoosh that came from the wand.

When Maddie opened her eyes, she saw a large purple tree standing in her backyard. The leaves sways in the wind, and Maddie was sure she saw two chipmunks up in the branches. "Oops. Let me try again."

"Wait, wait. You don't know how to use this?" Eoin's eyes widened.

"No, Mommy won't let me use it so I just have to guess." She spun it again, this time adding a few extra flicks. She opened her eyes to find Eoin's face buried in his hands. He wore a pink tutu and had fairy wings. "Oops."

"Can you please just—" Eoin snapped his fingers and made the tutu disappear. "Never mind. I'll do it."

Maddie pointed her wand at him, eyes narrowed. "You said it was my job. Let me do it."

Maybe if she pictured a bigger unicorn instead of picturing what she wanted to dress like for Halloween, it would work better. One more swish and then she pointed the wand at Muffins. She squealed in delight as Muffins shot up to be taller than Maddie.

"Why didn't you do that the first time?" Eoin tried to climb up on Muffins, but his legs were too short. He jumped, but his arms wouldn't reach over Muffins' back.

Maddie giggled and helped him up before running to find a footstool so she could climb up. She glanced down the street where William had gone and frowned. It would be sad if he didn't come, but the animals needed her right away. Maybe she could take him on the next adventure.

"Okay, so what do I do now? I don't know how to get to the fairy world." Maddie twisted so she could look at Eoin.

Eoin snapped his fingers and with a giant whoosh, they left Maddie's backyard.

# Chapter Three

With a loud pop, Maddie, Eoin, and Muffins landed in the fairy world. Maddie watched as small fairies flitted by, playing some of game. Trees grew all around them, and she could hear a small brook nearby.

"It's so magical here." Maddie moved to slide down off the unicorn, but Eoin grabbed her.

"We don't have time to run through the flowers, dance with the fairies, or whatever else you want to do. We have to find those animals and then leave again."

"Fine." Maddie stuck out her bottom lip, but settled in on Muffins' back. "Okay, so where do we go now? Do we get to see the fairy queen? I love her. She gave me strawberries last time we came. Megan said they're the best strawberries ever."

"No, the fairy queen's busy right now. She wouldn't be able to meet us. Besides, we have to go in the opposite direction." Eoin pointed to Maddie's right. Or her left. She could never remember.

Maddie leaned down to whisper in Muffins' ear. "Hey, I think you're supposed to go that way. Hey, can you hear me?"

"He can hear you. He just can't respond." Eoin held on tight around Maddie's waist as Muffins began trotting down the path.

Creatures leaped out of the way as Muffins went past. Some of them shook their fists in anger, while others scurried away. Maddie waved back at the angry creatures. Maybe later they would be willing to play. They probably knew some great hiding places.

At first it was exciting to ride along on a unicorn, but after passing tree after tree, she was bored and wanted to do something else. When they passed a fairy party where they were having tea, Maddie decided that it was time to take a break.

"It's time to eat I think. Hey, Muffins, I want a snack. Stop. No, I mean stop. Hey, do you know what stop means?" Maddie shouted.

Muffins suddenly slid to a stop, knocking Eoin off the back of him. Eoin rolled and rolled until he finally landed on his face in a mud puddle.

Maddie jumped down off of the unicorn and ran over to help him back up.

Mud covered his face, but Maddie helped him clean it off. "You should have held on tighter."

"Maybe you shouldn't have told the unicorn to stop so fast," he grumbled.

"But I wanted to go back to the fairy picnic. Come on." Maddie ran toward the clearing and nearly knocked over the small table they had set. "Hi! I'm Maddie. Can I have some tea too?"

Eoin caught up to Maddie, gasping for air. "You can't . . . eat their food. It will . . . make you sleep forever."

Maddie looked between Eoin and the fairies. "But it's just food. See? There are apples and sandwiches, and oh! Is that cake?"

One of the fairies handed her a piece of what looked like chocolate cake, but Eoin knocked it out of her hand. The fairy huffed and tried to hand her another piece, but Eoin stepped in front of her.

"No food. She's mortal. And not only that, she is Queen Megan's sister." Eoin glared down at all of them, his face red enough to match his beard.

All of the fairies gasped and flew away, leaving the tea party behind. Maddie reached forward to try just one apple, but Eoin took her by the shoulders and pushed her back toward Muffins.

Maddie shook free from Eoin and turned to him. "What's wrong with being Queen Megan's sister?"

"Nothing." Eoin snapped his fingers and a plate of sandwiches appeared in his hand. "Here. These are safe."

Maddie took one and bit into it. "If nothing is wrong with being her sister, then why did they run away?"

"Megan saved the fairy world. They wouldn't want to hurt you." Eoin took one of the sandwiches before offering the plate to Maddie. "I think we have to go up over the bridge over there and then go a little ways past that."

Maddie had two more sandwiches before she gave the plate back to Eoin. "A bridge? Is it a big bridge or a little bridge?"

"It's little. Or big. I guess it depends on who you are. I've never been there before." Eoin snapped his fingers and the plate disappeared.

"Wait, maybe Muffins wanted a sandwich." Mommy always told Maddie that Muffins only ate unicorn food. But maybe he would like a sandwich made by a leprechaun.

Eoin shook his head. "Muffins has grass. See?"

Muffins stood near the path, eating the grass on the side of the road. He looked up when Maddie stepped on a small twig, but went back to eating.

"We should let him eat. I know, let's go find a centaur. I've always wanted to see a centaur." Maddie whipped around, hoping there'd be one right there. "There are centaurs here, right? Or are they in our world? Did you know that Megan had to fight one? She said it was scary."

"They're only scary when they're in battle. And we won't be able to see one right now. They're off in the fields right now." Eoin tugged on Maddie's hand. "Come on, let's go save the animals. I need to get you back home before William realizes you're gone."

Maddie's heart was suddenly sad. She wished he was there with her. He would love to see the centaurs with her. Even if Eoin said they were far away.

Eoin snapped his fingers and appeared up on Muffin's back. He nearly lost his balance, but grabbed onto Muffins' neck. "Let's go."

"To find the centaurs?" Maddie brightened. Even if William couldn't be here, Maddie could see them herself and then tell William about them later.

"No, to—yes. To find the centaurs. If any happen to be over this way." Eoin scooted back so Maddie could climb on.

She whooped for joy and jumped to climb up on the unicorn. It took a few tries before she could finally get on, and then she shouted, "To the centaurs!"

# Chapter Four

The sun was hot, and Maddie was bored. This adventure in the fairy world was taking a lot longer than she wanted it to take. She had already counted all of the different kinds of flowers and trees, and made friends with a pixie. Eoin said that the faces the pixie was making were not very nice, but Maddie was sure that wasn't true.

Maddie had just started counting sunflowers when she suddenly sat up straight. "There's the bridge!"

Off in the distance, a tall stone bridge stood next to the brook. Maddie had seen bridges like these in picture books, and now she finally got to see one in person. As they got closer, she slid off Muffins' back and ran toward the stone walkway that led to the bridge.

A large growl from near the path made Maddie stop. What was that? Maddie looked behind her to see if Eoin was there yet, but he was still several feet away. Her stomach tied in knots.

"Hello?" Maddie called out. "Who's there?"

A large green creature stomped forward. He was taller than Daddy and carried a long club. He glared down at Maddie. "You may not pass this bridge."

Maddie huffed. "I have to cross the bridge. I need to save the animals."

"You may not pass," the troll grumbled.

Maddie placed her hands on her hips and made a mad face at him. "I need to go pass. The bad fairy has all of the animals and I need to save them."

The troll tapped its chin. "I will let you pass. But only if you answer my riddle. If you get it right, you can pass. If you get it wrong, then I'll send you away."

"I like riddles. My kindergarten teacher likes to tell them all the time. And I always get them right. William does too. Oh, he's my twin brother."

"Silence! You talk too much." The troll covered his ears. "I have to think."

Maddie zipped her lips so she wouldn't talk. While she waited for the troll to tell the riddle, she swayed back and forth. "Are you ready yet?"

"No." The troll scratched his head.

"How about now?" Maddie leaned forward, excited.

"No."

"I bet the answer is shoe." Maddie clapped her hands. "I like this game."

The troll grumbled. "No. It's not shoe. Here is the riddle. What goes up but never comes down?"

Maddie bit her lip. She remembered this one from her teacher. She turned to Eoin. "Do you know what it is?"

Eoin started to answer but the troll cut in.

"Only the girl can answer. No talking to the leprechaun." The troll folded his arms. "You must guess now, or I will send you away forever."

Maddie stared up at the sky, trying to think of the answer. She was distracted by the clouds as they floated by. Some had shapes like flowers and dragons, but most of them were just like the clouds she knew from home.

"Oh! I know what it is!" Maddie jumped up and down. "It's rain. It can go down into the ground, but it can't go back up."

The troll stomped his feet. "That was too easy. We need to do another one."

"That's not fair. You said I could get through if I answered a riddle." Maddie pulled out her wand. "Let me through or I'll turn you into a frog."

The troll laughed. "Your silly wand can't hurt me."

Maddie swung the wand in a large circle, then pointed it at the troll. With a *poof* the troll had lots of orange hair, just like a clown. "Are you going to let me through or not?"

"Get it off." The troll tried pulling on the hair, but it was good and stuck.

"Not until you help me." Maddie pointed the wand at him.

The troll held up his hands. "Okay. I will let you pass. But you must change me back."

Maddie waved her wand and pointed it at the troll. The orange hair disappeared, but it was replaced with a large bowtie. "There. I like it."

The troll grumbled again but moved out of the way. Maddie skipped up to him and gave him a hug before moving on.

"Watch out for the fairy. Don't let her know you're scared, so she'll catch you too," The troll called out.

Maddie ran back and gave him another hug. "Thank you, Mr. Troll."

As they walked over the bridge, Maddie peeked over the side and down at the water. It was clear, and she could see all sorts of fish swimming along.

"Let's go." Eoin pulled on her arm.

"But I want to see if there are mermaids." Maddie leaned clear over the side, but couldn't see any. "Maybe they're sleeping."

Eoin shook his head. "They don't come here often. They're all in Atlantis."

"Oh! I heard it's underwater. It's underwater, right? Can we go there next? I want to go. Megan told me no, but you'll take me, right? And maybe we can take William?" Maddie skipped around Eoin.

"We'll see. Let's just find the fairy."

They continued on while riding Muffins. Fairies flitted past them, and dryads cared for their trees. The sun was getting low when Muffins suddenly stopped. They couldn't get him to move forward, so Maddie slid off of him.

"How about I guide you?" Maddie rested her hand on Muffins' side and they walked slowly down the path. But soon Muffin refused to take another step. Maddie tried to grab hold of Muffins' horn, but it gave her a shock each time she tried to touch it.

"Never ever touch a unicorn's horn." Eoin snapped his fingers and a rope appeared in his hands. He made a quick knot and slipped it around Muffins' neck. "Ok, now try it."

"Come on. Just a little bit longer and then we can save the animals and you can have some carrots. You like carrots, remember?" Maddie tugged on the rope, but the unicorn refused to move. She finally let go of the harness and hugged Muffins. "No? Okay. Maybe you're just tired. We'll go first and then you can come later. Just don't run away or I can't get home."

Suddenly there was a snort behind Maddie. She turned to find a giant creature in front of her.

"Hi! How are you? I'm Maddie. This is Eoin. He's a leprechaun." Maddie held out her hand, but the creature just snorted again. "I didn't know there are dragons here."

"There aren't usually. He must be protecting something." Eoin tried to back up, but Maddie stood in place. "Maybe there's another way to get to the forest."

"But this is the fastest way and you keep telling me we need to hurry." Maddie walked around Eoin and walked closer to the dragon. "We need to get by. So, you just keep guarding and we'll be right back."

"Maddie, come on. He's not going to listen," Eoin whispered.

Maddie wanted to reach and touch the dragon's leathery skin, but by the way it stared down at her, she knew it was a very bad idea. "Doesn't he talk? I thought everything here talked."

Eoin snorted. "Who told you that?"

"No one. But Megan has lots of friends here and I just figured that everything talked." Maddie turned back. "Okay, Mr. Dragon, I know you don't talk, but maybe we can be friends anyway. You'd like that, right? We could have tea parties together, and go running through the bushes, and look for cloud shapes."

The dragon simply growled and lowered his head. Maddie's heart thumped loudly, but she wanted to get past. She took out her wand and pointed it at the dragon.

"Be nice, or I'll shrink you." Maddie didn't want to hurt it, but she also needed to get past him to save the animals.

The dragon scratched its feet on the ground, like it was going to pounce, and it snorted again. Just as it started toward her, Maddie flicked the wand at the dragon and a flash of light appeared. Maddie had to close her eyes because it was so bright.

When she finally opened her eyes, she giggled. The dragon was now smaller than Eoin. This was too much for the dragon and it yelped, running off into the trees.

## Chapter Five

Y ou're really getting the hang of that wand. Well, except for the troll's bowtie. Unless you did that on purpose." Eoin went back to Muffins. "I think he'll be fine now. He was probably scared of the dragon. They know when danger is around."

Maddie climbed up and helped Eoin. "I don't think the dragon will scare anyone anymore. Do you think the fairy is still with the animals? Maybe we can save them without having to see her."

"I don't know. We'll see." Eoin was quiet until they got farther into the forest. "I think we're close. I don't hear anything, and usually it's full of animal sounds."

They continued down the path until they came to a fork in the road. Maddie looked down each path, trying to decide which way to go. One was looked scary, and the other one had a stone wall that ran along the path.

"Which way do we go?" Maddie stared at the sign, but the words were not the same as she had learned in kindergarten.

Eoin stood next to her. "I'm not sure I wish Da would have given me more information."

"Wait, what's that sound?" Maddie searched through the trees, but didn't see anything.

Eoin listened, then shook his head. "I don't know. It's like all of the noises of the forest are in one spot."

Maddie climbed off the unicorn. "I think it's coming from over there."

Eoin dropped down off of Muffles and landed on his back with an *ooph*. "Let's go! And keep your wand out."

Maddie and Eoin ran through the forest, jumping over the vines that covered the ground. Maddie tripped over a branch and fell into the vines. She jumped up and kept running even though her knee and hands hurt.

The trees opened up into a big valley. In the center was a throne like you'd find in a castle, and on the throne was a beautiful fairy. Her wings were black, and her dress was dark purple. Behind her was a large cage filled with every animal Maddie could think of.

The fairy gave Maddie a mean look. "Leave my forest at once."

"This isn't your forest. And you need to let the animals go." Maddie held out her wand. "This was from King Jared and he would be mad if he knew that you were being mean."

The fairy laughed. "Jared is no longer king, so it doesn't matter what he wants to do."

Maddie huffed. "He's not king, but he gave me this wand. Do you know whose wand this is?"

"How did you get that?" The fairy stood, her eyes wide. "That wand was locked away in a castle far, far away."

"I didn't get it. My sister did. Now, please let the animals go. They're crying." Maddie's eyes filled with tears while she listened to the calls they made.

The fairy stared at her before bursting into tears. "I can't let them go. I want them as friends."

Maddie's jaw dropped. "You took them so you would have friends? But that's not how it works. You have to be nice to them."

"But I don't know how. I was raised to be a dark fairy, not a nice fairy." She covered her face with her hands.

Maddie brightened. "I can be your friend. My mommy taught me to be nice."

The fairy sniffed. "Really?"

"Yes, but you have to let the animals go." Maddie walked past the fairy and tried to open the cage where the animals had been locked up. She pointed the wand at the lock and then flicked the wand toward it.

The lock opened, and Maddie turned to the fairy. "I'm going to let them go now, okay?"

The fairy nodded, sniffling.

Birds, cats, snakes, and even little snails flowed out of the cage. Maddie waved at them as they left, back to their home, then walked back over to the fairy.

"My name is Maddie. What's yours?" She held a hand out.

"Bluebelle." She wiped her eyes. "I have never had a friend before. What does it mean?"

"We play together." Maddie jumped up and down. "I know! Eoin told me we could see centaurs. Want to come with us?"

Eoin smacked his forehead. "We can't go see them. They're too far away."

"But you did the snappy thing to get us here. You can do that to get us the centaurs, right?" Maddie scrambled up onto Muffin's back. "Let's go!"

Bluebelle helped Eoin up. "I'll help."

She waved her hands, and the ground disappeared beneath them, then suddenly reappeared. Instead of the trees and bushes that Maddie had grown used to, there are large, open fields of grain and other plants. Centaurs walked through with a shovel in their hands.

Eoin sighed. "Can we go now? Your mom must be getting worried about."

"Wait, you're leaving?" Bluebell's lip quivered. "We just started playing."

Maddie looked between Eoin and Bluebelle. "Eoin is right. I need to get home. Maybe we can play tomorrow?"

"That would be great." Bluebelle pulled off her necklace. "I want you to have this. That way you, can find me when you come back."

"Thank you." Maddie put it on and held tight as Eoin snapped his finger to take them back home.

# Chapter Six

"William! William, I'm home!" Maddie ran around the side of the house to find her brother. He sat in the sandbox, playing with his dump trucks.

"Where'd you go? I couldn't find you in the house." William stood and wiped the sand off his pants.

Maddie slipped the wand into her belt. "We went on an adventure. There were centaurs, and fairies, and pixies. Oh! And I found a castle in the clouds. The shapes are much better in the fairy world."

"Better than my pirate ship? That was cool." William picked up his sword.

"Yes, I could see the windows and everything. Next time you can come with me and see them for yourself."

William paused. "Did you really see centaurs?"

"Yes, they were working in the fields. And they were big!" Maddie held her arms out to show him just how big they were.

"Cool. Maybe we can go back sometime." William held up his sword. "Do you think there's anyone there I can fight?"

Maddie rolled her eyes. "It's the fairy world. Of course there will be."

"Maddie! William! It's time for dinner," their mom called.

Maddie turned to find that Eoin and Muffins had disappeared. She shrugged and followed William inside. She could play with Bluebell tomorrow.

# About Jaclyn Weist

Jaclyn is an Idaho farm girl who grew up loving to read. She developed a love for writing at a young age and published her first book in 2013. She met her husband, Steve, at BYU, and they have six happy, crazy children who encourage her to keep writing. After owning a bookstore and running away to have adventures in Australia, they settled back down in their home in Utah. Jaclyn now spends her days herding her kids to various activities and trying to remember what she was supposed to do next. Her books include the Lost in a Fairy Tale Series ~ Endless, Timeless, and Fearless; Magicians of the Deep; Leana; Keela; and the Luck series, which helped feed her obsession with all things Irish. You can learn more about her at www.jaclynweist.com

# About Heidi Weist

Heidi is a fun-loving girl just like Maddie. She loves soccer, dance, and playing with friends. Maddie Saves the Day is her first book, but definitely won't be her last.

91527235R00033

Made in the USA
San Bernardino, CA
22 October 2018